A Trip to the Dentist

Fran Campbell

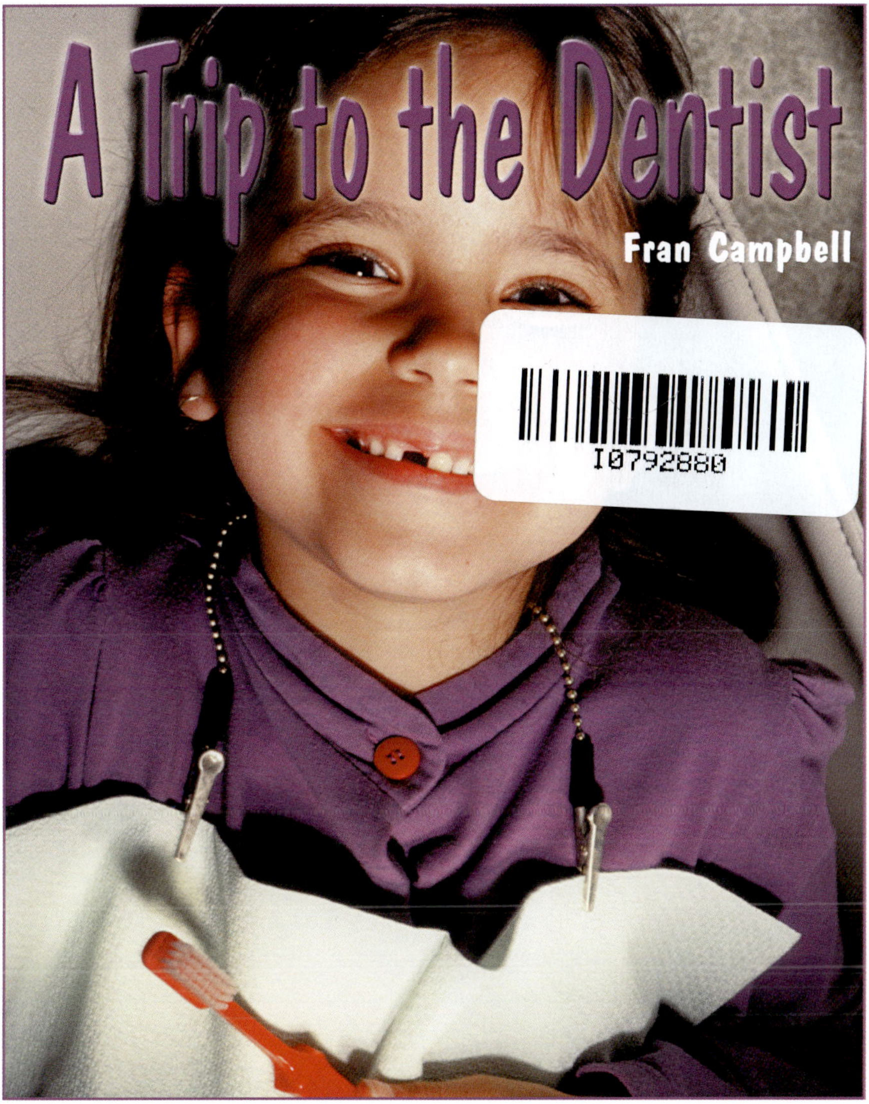

Rosen REAL READERS

The Rosen Publishing Group, Inc.

New York

Strong, **healthy** teeth help you eat, talk, and smile. Brushing your teeth every day keeps your teeth clean and healthy.

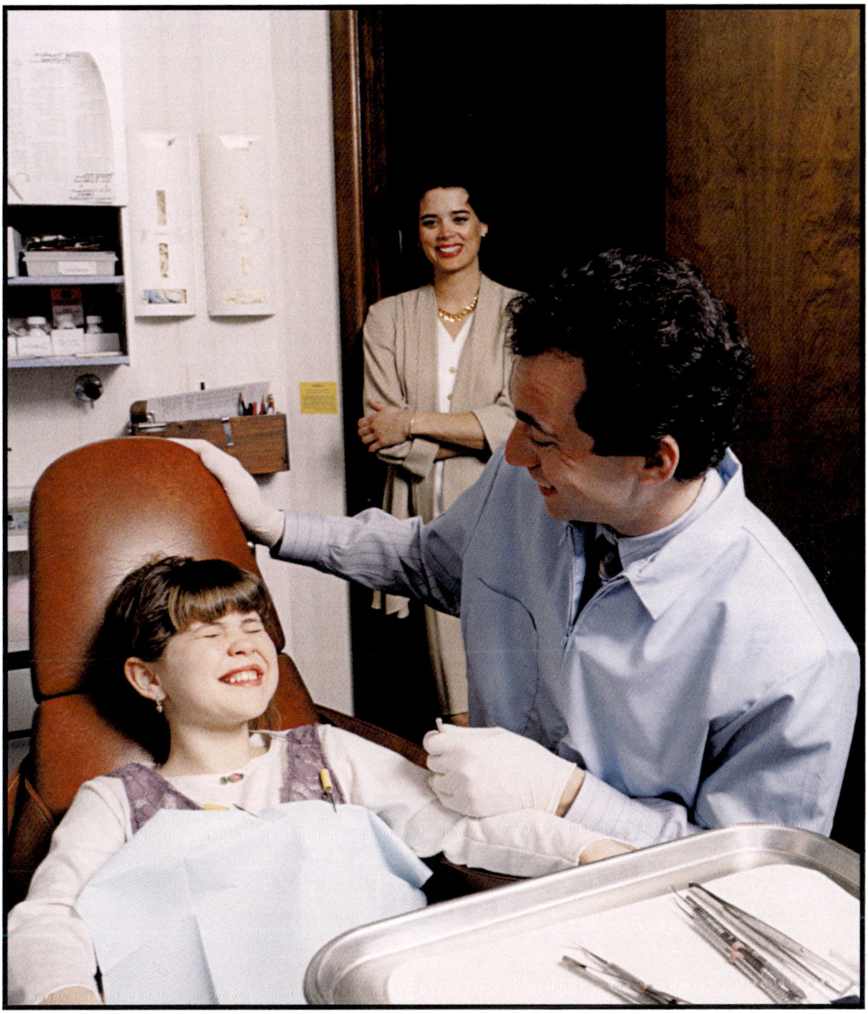

The dentist also keeps your teeth healthy. A dentist is a **doctor** who takes care of your teeth.

When you go to the dentist, you wait for your turn in the **waiting room**. You can read a book or play with a toy while you wait.

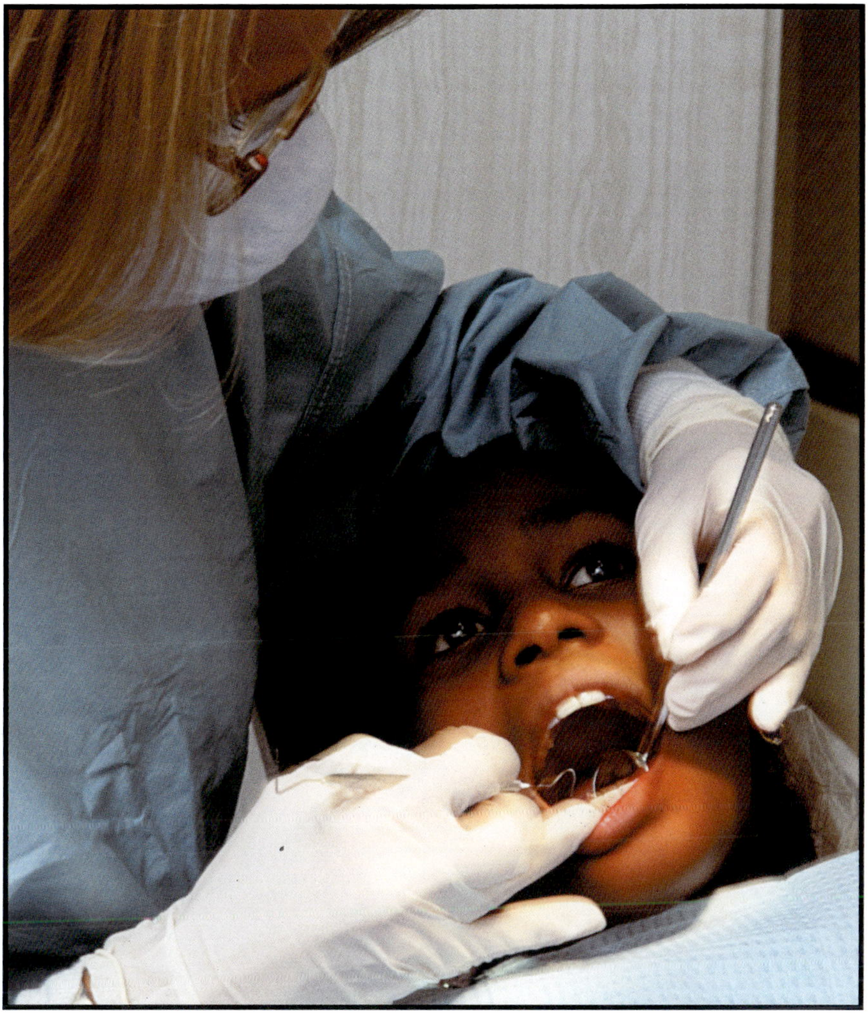

When it is your turn, you sit in a big chair. The dentist looks at your teeth and **gums** to make sure they are healthy.

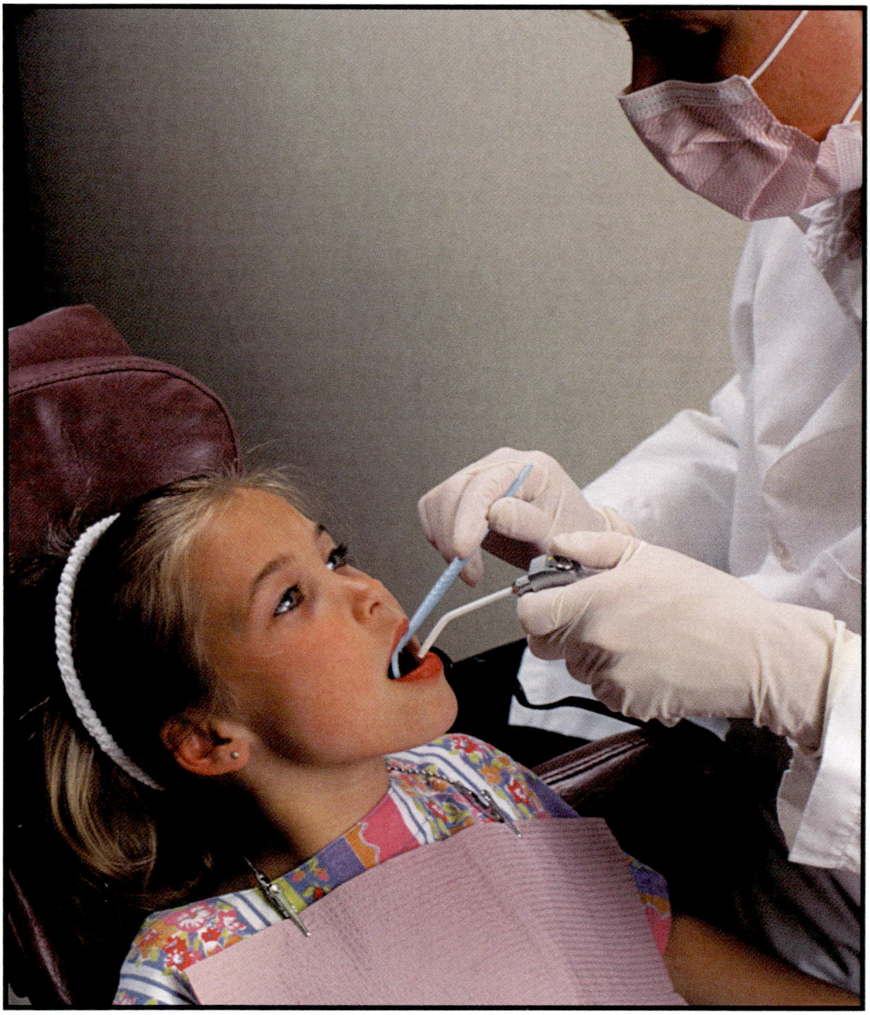

The dentist cleans your teeth with special **tools**.

The dentist takes **X rays** of your teeth. The X rays show the dentist if there is anything wrong with your teeth.

The dentist shows you how to take care of your teeth. The dentist shows you how to brush your teeth the right way.

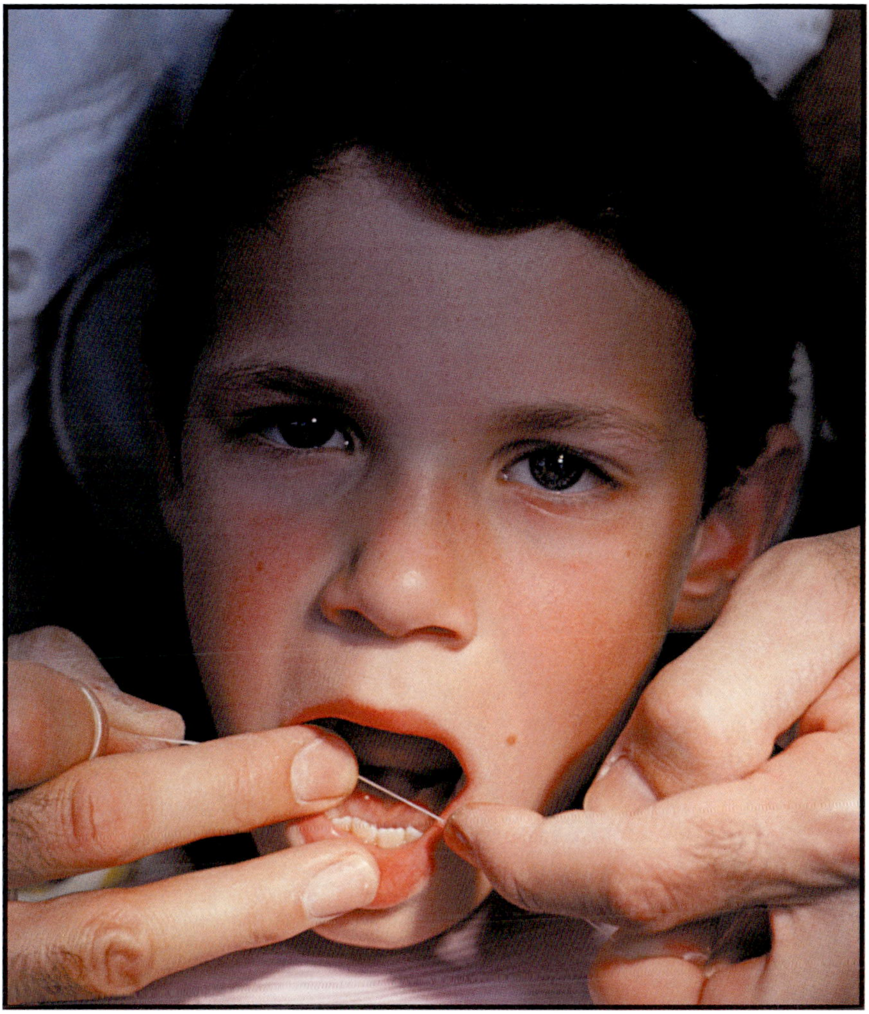

The dentist also shows you how to **floss** your teeth. This helps you clean between your teeth.

The dentist may tell you to drink milk to keep your teeth strong. Foods with a lot of sugar, like candy, make your teeth weak.

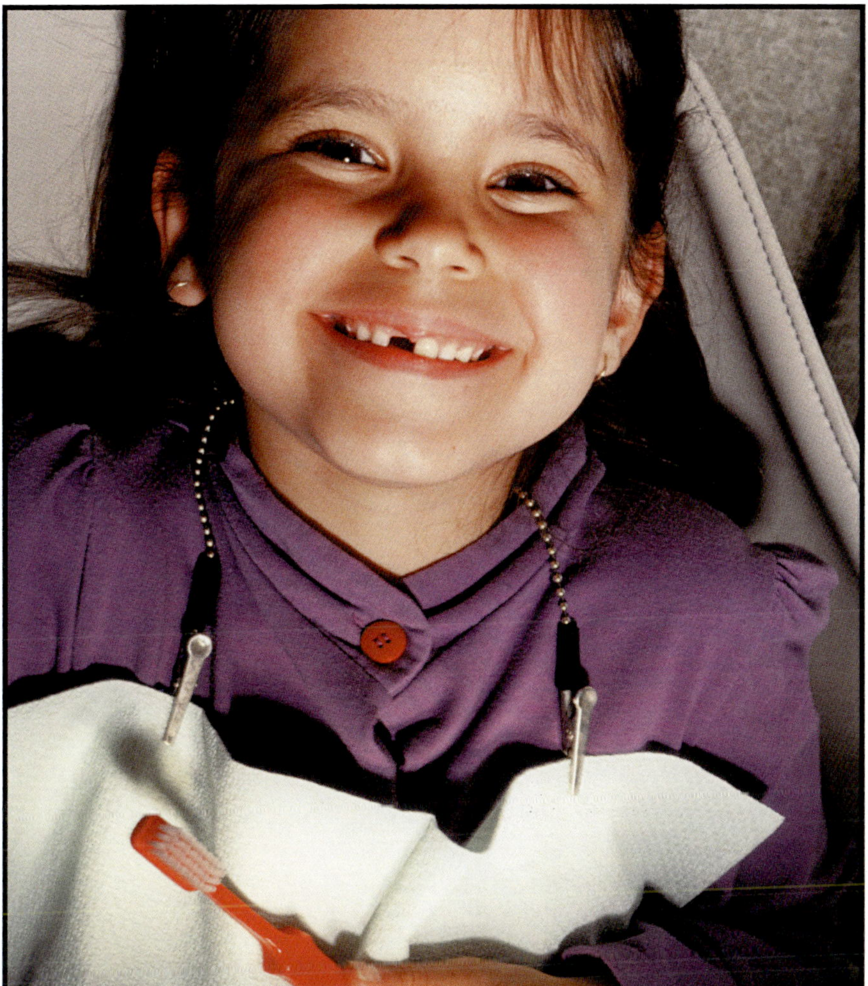

The dentist may even give you a new **toothbrush** before you leave!

Glossary

doctor	Someone who is trained to make sick people well.
floss	To use a waxy string to clean between your teeth.
gum	The soft, pink skin in your mouth that your teeth grow out of.
healthy	Well or strong.
tool	Something that is used to make a job easier.
toothbrush	A small brush used to clean your teeth and gums.
waiting room	A room in a doctor's office where you wait until the doctor can see you.
X ray	A picture of part of the inside of your body.